SWARM OF FLYING EYEBALLS

GINA RANALLI

deadite
press

DEADITE PRESS
P.O. BOX 10065
PORTLAND, OR 97296
www.DEADITEPRESS.com

AN ERASERHEAD PRESS COMPANY
www.ERASERHEADPRESS.com

ISBN: 978-1-62105-302-6

Swarm of Flying Eyeballs copyright © 2009, 2019 by Gina Ranalli

Cover design by Deadite Press

Printed in the USA.

Dedicated to Lee Widener, a great friend without whom this edition would not exist. I'm so glad we survived both our marriage and divorce. Love you, buddy.

SWARM OF FLYING EYEBALLS

1

Ron watched the children file off the school bus, chittering like monkeys, as he stood at the edge of the blueberry field, squinting in the early morning sun. Summer school kids, he knew, as he plucked a freshly picked berry from the cup of one dirty hand and popped it into his mouth, chewing thoughtfully. Didn't seem right to him somehow. Summer school kids getting a field trip. What was up with that? In his day, you got stuck with summer school, then you spent every waking moment either studying or getting your ass whooped for failing the regular school year to begin with. There had been no field trips back then. Hell no. Just sweltering classrooms and pissed off teachers who wanted you to just sit there and shut up.

He oughta know. He'd ended up in summer school pretty much every year of his life, until he finally dropped out at fourteen and had hit the road in search of work.

Now thirty-one, he worked picking berries in the summer. The money sucked, but he liked being outdoors, watching his skin turn golden brown, flexing the ropey muscles of his arms as he carried bushel after bushel from the field to the trucks, heaving them up into the beds as if they weighed no more than a newborn baby.

As far as Ron was concerned, life was pretty good. Particularly when he was working. He ate a few more blueberries before turning back to the field and doing his best to ignore the kids. There was work to be done.

2

Hoping she didn't get too dirty, Natalie followed her classmates into the blueberry field, grimacing slightly at the thought that her new white sneakers might get scuffed or muddy. She didn't understand why they had to take a dumb field trip anyway. But, then again, the fact that she was in summer school at all was pretty ridiculous in the first place.

Extra credit, her dad had said. Graduate early, he'd said. Youngest pro on the circuit, he'd said.

Natalie liked the sound of that well enough. She knew she was already the best tennis player to ever come out of Washington state and she was only twelve. All this extra work off the court was nothing but a drag. Especially when it served no purpose, like right now. They should all have been back at school, reading Lord of the Flies or practicing algebra. Not here under the boiling sun, being handed a little plastic basket to load up with blueberries.

Sighing, she took her basket and wandered into the field, absently plucking a berry from a bush now and then, but mostly just wandering, watching her step and lost in thought, wishing her arm was strong enough to master a single handed backswing. More weight training was in order, she thought.

"No eating the berries," Mr. O'Brien called to the kids. "They need to be washed first."

Natalie looked around and saw that several of the other kids were eating berries, despite being warned not to. She shook her head in disgust. They weren't exactly brainiacs, this bunch.

"Don't forget about insecticide," Mr. O'Brien further warned. "Remember we talked about that."

Rolling her eyes, Natalie swatted at a bee that had flown too close to her face and made her way further into the blueberry brambles.

3

"Quit hitting your brother!"

Lisa ignored her mother shouting from the living room and slugged Matt in the arm again. "Give me that, you pervert!" she snarled.

Matt held her bag over her head. Despite being two years younger than his seventeen year old sister, he was almost a full foot taller. "You have tampons in here!" he jeered, swinging her bag back and forth, just out of her reach.

"You're a pus-bag!" Lisa said and punched him solidly in the belly.

Matt doubled over with a loud huff of air and Lisa snatched the bag from him, debating on whether or not to give him another whack for good measure.

"Lisa!" her mother screeched from the living room. "You mind what I say!"

Frowning, Lisa walked away from Matt and went into the living room where her mother—all six hundred pounds of her—sat on the couch, the television in front of her advertising some new brand of toilet cleaner while a pretty actress grinned from ear to ear, apparently delighted to be scrubbing a filthy, germ-infested toilet.

"He wouldn't give me my bag," Lisa said.

"That doesn't give you the right to hit him," her mother said, shifting her weight slightly, her eyes riveted to the television set. "Violence is never the answer."

Lisa's frown deepened. She recalled a time before her mother grew into the behemoth she was and would chase Lisa around with a ping-pong ball paddle, swatting at the little girl's behind while shouting curses and threats.

"Whatever," Lisa said. "I'm going out."

"Where to?"

"I'm meeting Stacy at her place."

Shirley scoffed. "Get me a Coke."

Resisting the urge to argue, Lisa pursed her lips and went to do as she was told. Sometimes it was just easier.

She was happy to see that Matt was no longer in the kitchen but was also suspicious as to where he may have gone. She grabbed a Coke from the refrigerator and then paused at the foot of the stairs leading up to the bedrooms. "You'd better not be in my room, Matt!" She hollered menacingly.

"Screw you," came his reply.

His voice was muffled, coming from behind a closed door. Probably the bathroom, Lisa assumed, and continued back to the living room to hand over the Coke.

Her mother took the can, popped it open and drank half of it in a single swallow before letting out a large belch. "Rub my feet," she commanded, her eyes still never wavering from the TV.

"Mom!" Lisa cried. "I told you, I'm going out!"

"Where's Matthew?"

"Probably playing with himself."

"What?"

"Upstairs. Can I please just go? I don't want to be late."

Shirley waved the girl away and Lisa took this as permission to get while the getting was good.

As she was closing the front door behind her, she grimaced slightly at the sound of her mother screeching her brother's name.

4

Leaning against the front of the school bus, Travis lit a smoke and watched the kids running around in the blueberry field. He was tired, a bit hung-over and just wanted the day to end, even though it had barely begun.

He'd thought the bus driving gig would be an easy one—and it was, for the most part. What he hadn't counted on was having to deal with a bunch of screaming kids when his head was pounding and his stomach was trying to climb up his throat and empty itself on the hot tarmac.

If only that dork O'Brien would just mind his own business, Travis could smoke his cigarette and then climb into the bus and snooze for a bit. But O'Brien would report him for sure. The guy was a tool. Travis knew it and the kids knew it too. Hell, everyone in town knew it. Norm O'Brien would rat out his own mother if he suspected her of cheating at Bingo.

"Stay where I can see you!" O'Brien shouted at the students, though all twelve of them were within easy sight of the guy.

Travis snorted and looked down at his boots, chuffing smoke from his nostrils. Any second he expected O'Brien to give him grief for smoking in the first place, at which time Travis intended to tell him to go pound sand. He was eighteen, legal smoking age, and if his own parents couldn't stop him from doing it, than neither would his old nemesis, O'Brien.

He was stomping on the butt of his cigarette a

minute later when he heard the scream. Looking up, he was surprised to see some of the kids out in the middle of the blueberry field, each carrying their own little green plastic basket to gather the berries in. Those little buggers move fast when they want to, he thought. Someone else screamed, but Travis couldn't tell who it was. At that age, some of the boys still sounded like girls when they squealed like that.

Probably some kid was pelting another with berries. Travis figured that's what he'd be doing if he was being forced to pick berries this early in the morning.

O'Brien did some hollering of his own, telling the kids to settle down. "You're not out here to horse around!" The teacher yelled. "Any more behavior like that and you're going back on the bus!"

Travis wondered why they were out here, if not to horse around. He saw one of the field hands making his way around the waist-high bushes, heading for one of the kids who'd wandered off by herself.

As Travis watched, the girl bent down and disappeared from sight, maybe to pick berries growing close to the ground.

Then came another scream and the field hand rushed towards the place where the girl had been.

A silent moment passed when everyone's attention was on the two-man and girl-and then their yells mingled and both popped up and took off running, heading straight for the bus.

Straightening up, Travis frowned, trying to make out what the two were screaming. He knew he must have misheard them, but for a second there it sounded as if they were both shouting about eyeballs.

5

Hearing the girl scream like that gave Ron the willies.

He took off in the direction of the kid, hoping against hope that she hadn't encountered a wasp's ground nest. He was deathly afraid of wasps-allergic to any kind of sting-but still, he couldn't just let the kid fend for herself. It was obvious the teacher wasn't about to do anything. The guy was still just standing at the edge of the field, hands on hips, a scowl on his face.

Ron shoved his way through the bushes, glancing around frantically until the girl popped up about ten feet to his right.

"Are you okay?" he asked. "Did you get stung?"

The girl was a skinny thing, kind of tomboyish, with short dark hair, wearing a green and white baseball jersey. Her dark eyes met his, wide and frightened, as she slowly shook her head and pointed down with a tiny trembling finger.

Slowing his pace, but still walking towards her, Ron asked, "Is it wasps?"

"I...no, but..." The girl trailed off, looking down at the ground.

Ron swallowed a lump in his throat. "Then what—"

The girl jumped as something—some things—burst up from where she was standing. Dozens of flying blue orbs with what appeared to be red tails zipping into the air, moving too fast for Ron to get a good look them.

"What the...?"

The orbs changed direction at the sound of his

voice, flew towards him and stopped a couple feet from his face, hovering in mid-air.

His brain scrambled frantically, trying to make sense of what he was seeing. Flying blueberries? But how could that be? It was impossible. Unless...

Unless something had burrowed into them, but what? Wasps? But those red things...the tails...

Ron's theory stopped in its tracks when the orb closest to him suddenly opened, the blue skin peeling back like two eyelids and he saw that that was exactly what they were.

Eyelids.

Watery pink surrounded a purple iris with a small black pupil as it stared directly at him and Ron's scream was even louder than the girl's had been, causing every floating eye to spring open, swiveling their Cyclops gazes towards him.

"EYEBALLS!" Ron shrieked, turning tail and sprinting away from them, arms flailing.

"EYEBALLS!" the girl agreed, bolting after Ron and then passing him, aiming for the bus and her classmates. "They're all eyeballs!"

6

Legs pumping, Natalie dropped her little basket and raced as fast as she could, intending to jump into the bus and drive the thing away herself if she had to.

But, that plan wasn't meant to be. Instead, as soon as she broke free of the blueberry bushes, O'Brien stepped into her path, hands on hips, scowling down at her.

Natalie broke right, but her teacher was quick, grabbing her around the waist and stopping her escape.

"Let me go!" Natalie cried, struggling in O'Brien's grasp. "The eyeballs are gonna get me!"

O'Brien sighed as though the weight of the world was on his shoulders while simultaneously tightening his grip on her. "Stop it!" he snapped. "What's wrong with you? Do you think this is funny, making a scene like this?"

Still screaming, Ron swept past them, his face pale, his eyes stretched wide with terror.

"They're coming! They're coming! Hurry! We have to get out of here."

Without pausing to explain what he meant by this ominous warning, the field hand kept right on going, past the few children who had cautiously wandered over to see what the commotion was about and then right by the bus as well, taking off down the middle of the street, throwing glances back over his shoulder as if he expected to find demons from Hell in hot pursuit.

O'Brien rolled his eyes before looking down at the still squirming Natalie. "Did that man do something to you?" he asked. "Did he touch you somewhere?"

"What?" Natalie sounded offended. "No! Let me

go! The eyeballs are coming!"

"Oh, the eyeballs. Of course. Why didn't you say so?" O'Brien winked reassuringly at the children gathered around. "Beware the scary eyeballs, kids!"

Natalie stomped down as hard as she could on O'Brien's right foot, causing the man to let out a loud yelp and loosen his grip on the girl. "You brat!" he yelled, releasing her in order to hop around on one foot. "You spoiled little brat!"

Free and running towards the bus, that last comment was almost enough to make Natalie stop and give that dill hole a good telling off, but she'd seen the blueberries flutter to life, shivering on their stems and dropping to the ground. At first she'd assumed they were over-ripe and had knelt over to examine them. They looked like perfectly fine, average, every day blueberries, until the moment when tiny fin-like protrusions emerged from the sides and began flapping like wings, propelling the fruit into the air.

That had been weird enough, but then the man had come over and said something and…

Natalie reached the bus and pounded up the stairs into it, before turning to face outside again. The bus driver—that cute blond guy with the curly hair and green eyes-strolled towards the side of the bus, looking in at her with curiosity. "What's up?" he asked once he'd reached the door.

Natalie opened her mouth but abruptly snapped it shut again. Behind the cute bus driver, clouds of those weird blueberries were rising up, hovering above the bushes as if unsure of how to proceed now that they'd awakened. Unsure, that was, until they somehow heard something—voices—at which time, even from a distance, Natalie could see the eyes springing open as blueberries spun around to focus on whoever happened to be speaking.

7

I hate this town, Lisa thought as she walked down a mostly deserted Main Street. Berryville was too small, too dull and definitely too lame, as far as she was concerned. Main Street itself was only a few blocks long, lined with a hardware store, a few clothing shops, a pizza place, an ice cream parlor, and a video rental store, which literally still carried VHS tapes only. Beyond those exciting tourist stops were a couple of banks and a place that repaired typewriters.

Lisa groaned just thinking about it. Berryville was stuck in the dark ages. It may as well be the 80's as far as her hometown was concerned.

At the end of Main, she took a left onto Franklin and was almost immediately in the boonies. The middle school was down this way, but beyond that it was mostly a quiet residential neighborhood, flanked by the Berryville Blueberry Farm.

Crinkling her nose at the mere thought of blueberries, Lisa thought that that might be the best reason for getting out of Berryville yet. If she never ate another blueberry for as long as she lived, it would be too soon. For that matter, she didn't think she'd be that disappointed to never even hear the word or see the berry ever again either.

Claim to fame my butt. There's probably about 2,000 people total who've ever even heard of Berryville. And that includes everyone who lives here.

Shouting caused Lisa to look up from the sidewalk, her silent lamenting about being born into a small dead-end town interrupted by a man's far-off voice.

She rolled her eyes, assuming it was just some domestic dispute in one of the small tract houses she was passing on her way to Stacy's place. Some people in Berryville tended to drink quite a bit to pass the time and as a result, most of the townsfolk were accustomed to shouting matches between family members.

It wasn't until she was able to make out the words that she suspected it might be more than just a squabble between husband and wife. To Lisa, it sounded more like someone had slipped a groove, as her father used to like to say.

This wasn't entirely unheard of in Berryville either. Not everyone could take the small town boredom with grace and every so often someone would go crazy and have to be carted off to the asylum over in Milton.

"The blueberries are eyeballs!" a man shouted, the voice off to her right, coming from the backyard of Mr. and Mrs. Moore, an old couple that owned one of the clothing shops on Main.

Lisa paused, her brow creased. It didn't sound like old man Moore and a moment later she discover why.

Bolting from around the side of the Moore house came a younger man. Lisa thought he looked familiar but couldn't quite place him.

The yelling man paused when he reached the front lawn, looking down the street in the direction of the farm, his face pinched with fear.

Lisa followed his gaze with her own, but saw nothing unusual. When she returned her attention to the man, she was distressed to discover that he had not only noticed her but was already making his way towards her.

"They're all eyeballs now," he said loudly, reaching a dirty hand out to her, despite being a good twenty feet away. "They all turned into eyeballs."

8

Travis saw the girl's wide frightened blue eyes and assumed it was because of her tussle with O'Brien. She was looking over his head, probably because O'Brien was headed towards the bus this very second, most likely with a look of fury on his face.

"Don't worry about it," Travis said. "He's full of hot air."

When the girl ignored him—apparently didn't even hear him—Travis turned and saw what she saw. Not O'Brien. He was still standing by the vast field of blueberry bushes, his back to the bus, evidently watching what everyone was watching: the strange swirling clouds shifting above the field.

From a distance, Travis took the clouds for insects of some kind. Insects with…were those tails? What kind of round flying bug has a tail that long?

"We have to get out of here," the girl said quietly. As Travis turned back to her, she was suddenly shouting at her classmates.

"Get on the bus! Come on! Come on! Hurry!"

The urgency in her voice made Travis's heart thud in his chest. Confused, he once more looked back at the fields and saw the clouds moving forward, aiming directly at the kids, some of whom had already decided they didn't like the looks of those weird flying things and were headed for the bus.

They're not moving fast enough, Travis thought as he studied the strange bugs—if that's what they were.

Eyeballs, the girl had called them.

Several seconds passed, some of the children still walking towards the bus, casting worried glances over their shoulders.

"Where do you think you're going?" O'Brien hollered at them, his back to the field. The teacher's face was flushed with frustration; he looked like he was ready to blow a gasket, unable to understand why the children were being so disobedient today.

Travis, like the kids, ignored O'Brien, his gaze still focused on the swarms of bugs.

But, no. Not bugs at all.

The girl was right.

Eyes widening in fear, Travis shouted at the children. "RUN!"

9

"I saw them," Ron told Lisa as he approached her from the opposite side of the street. "You don't want to go down there. We have to get away. Everyone has to get away."

The teenager backed up a step or two and her expression was unmistakable: she thought Ron was loony toons.

"Whatever you say, buddy," she told him.

"It's true," he nodded frantically, holding up his hands in an attempt to convey that he meant her no harm. Was, in fact, trying to save her. "Flying eyeballs. I think it was the new insecticide, maybe mixed with that fertilizer that came from out of state. I don't know. But they're dangerous. I can feel it. You'd feel it too if you saw one. If you looked it in…" He swallowed. "In the eye."

"Maybe you should go sleep it off," the girl told him and began walking briskly away, heading in the very direction Ron had just told her to avoid.

He moved quickly, seizing the opportunity when she'd turned her back to him. He rushed forward, gripping her arm hard. "Aren't you listening? You can't go down there! They'll…hurt you."

Lisa jerked her arm free. "I swear to God, I'll scream if you touch me again. Just leave me alone."

Ron could see her sizing him up, studying his dirty hands and clothes, probably mistaking him for a homeless person. "I work at the farm," he tried to explain. "I saw them! And so did the little girl."

"The little girl." Lisa had begun walking down the street again, trying to quicken her pace. "Right."

When he realized that she wasn't listening—didn't want to listen—Ron stopped, unsure of how to proceed. Should he just grab the teen? Carry her in the opposite direction, away from those things, whatever they were.

But, of course, deep down he already knew what they were. An abomination, straight from Hell. Demons of some kind, probably.

Ron had never been particularly religious, but he'd been raised in a Baptist household and had heard the warnings of damnation his entire life. He'd never given them much thought, blowing off the ravings of his parents the way most kids do.

But now he knew they were right. Hell was here for sure. He'd seen it with his own two eyes.

"May God be with you," he called after the retreating girl. Words he'd never expected to hear coming from his own mouth.

He watched her for a moment longer and then turned away and began jogging up the street with no particular destination in mind. Just away.

10

"Come on," Natalie yelled. She couldn't understand why most of the kids were still just staring at her, looking like a bunch of dumb robots that'd been switched off.

The blond bus driver suddenly shouted, urging everyone to get on the bus and she felt like hugging him because finally—FINALLY—people seemed to be paying attention, looking back at the field. Natalie could see the color draining from the faces of several of her classmates while others frowned, more puzzled than frightened.

Only Mr. O'Brien didn't move, didn't turn to see where the blond guy was pointing.

The kids all rushed towards the bus at once, some of them screaming and at first Natalie was confused by their abrupt change in behavior. That was, until she glanced up and saw that the swarms had grown thicker still, all of the small ones merging into one mass of moving darkness.

"Holy crap," she whispered. "They're headed right for us."

The driver quickly stepped aside as a dozen kids scrambled up the steps of the bus, a few of the bigger ones trying to shove their way forward.

O'Brien was at last enraged enough to start for the bus as well, completely oblivious to the swarm that silently whooshed through the air and engulfed him.

It seemed to Natalie that the eyeballs had had every intention of just flying by her teacher, passing him the

24

way most insects will pass a boulder on their way to a flower garden.

But then O'Brien must have seen what they were and he screamed. It was easily the loudest scream Natalie had ever heard and it didn't sound like a man at all. Maybe an animal, but not a man. Nothing human.

And that's when the transformed blueberries took notice of him, swinging easily in the direction of that inhuman voice, their strange red tails curled up over what she couldn't help but think of as their heads.

Scorpions, she thought vaguely. They sting like scorpions.

Mr. O'Brien began to thrash, doing his best to swat the creatures away, but it was obvious the fight was going to be over before it began.

Seconds later and the man was on his knees, and then he'd disappeared from sight completely.

Everyone had fallen silent, peering out the bus windows as their teacher crumpled to the ground making the most horrendous sounds anyone had ever heard. It was a moment that seemed to stretch into infinity—even the air seemed to be holding its breath.

Natalie stood poised, still standing on the top step with the bus driver below her. When she spoke to him, she was surprised not only at what she said, but also at the calmness with which she said it: "We should go while they're distracted."

The driver looked up at her; his gorgeous eyes blinked once. "Yeah," he agreed. "Let's go."

11

Relieved that that weird guy wasn't following her, Lisa let herself relax a bit. She'd looked back several times and had seen him take off in the opposite direction, so she was pretty sure she was safe. He was no longer in sight and she could get on with her day.

The crap I have to put up with, she thought as she began rummaging around in her purse while she walked. First my stupid family and then that guy. Am I just a freak magnet or what?

She found the lip gloss she'd been searching for and began to apply it, wondering if she should give Stacy a call from her cell to let her know she was just a few minutes away. She was coming up on the Berryville farm, could see a school bus parked on the curb about a quarter of a mile up the road.

Knowing it was most likely Travis's bus, she quickened her step, her lips curling into a smile. This was a nice surprise. She hadn't expected to see him until tonight. In fact, maybe could hop aboard and get a quick lift from him. That was, unless that jerk O'Brien had some exception to it, which he most likely would. Man, she hated that guy.

From where she was, she could clearly hear the kids screaming. They were probably messing around, throwing berries at each other and running every which way. The thought made her smile widen, knowing that O'Brien was most certainly turning 100 shades of red. There was nothing he hated more than kids disobeying him, unless it was kids just having a good time.

As she drew closer to the scene, her smile slipped a notch as she watched the kids suddenly race towards the bus, all clambering to get on. And that was Travis standing by the door, ushering them up. She could tell by the way the sun was glinting off his blond hair, making him look positively angelic, a glowing halo covering his head.

The thought amused her slightly—Travis was certainly no angel when he got her alone in his beat-up old Buick-but then the realization that she wasn't hearing squeals of delight came to her. No, that wasn't the sound of kids having fun. It was the sound of kids being terrorized.

No longer amused or smiling, Lisa broke into a run. She had no idea what was going on, but when she heard a man begin to wail in agony, she knew that she probably wouldn't be seeing Stacy today after all.

12

Once all the kids were on the bus, Travis climbed up and swung the door closed just as several eyeballs flew at them, smashing into the glass with small thuds.

To his amazement, the creatures didn't collide with the glass, explode or simply fall out of sight. What they did instead, was stick.

Travis watched in disgust as what looked to be the thing's iris pushed forward, forming some sort of suction ring, adhering it to the glass.

Behind Travis, Natalie peered around his body and said, "Gross."

He'd swear something crawled the length of his spine then and it was through shear force of will that he turned away from the door, gently moving Natalie back, and took his seat behind the wheel.

More eyes pelted the side of the bus and as more stuck to the windows, more of the kids saw the creatures and began to shout, scream or cry.

There was one particular blood-curdling scream that made Travis whirl in his seat before he could even start the engine.

Towards the middle of the bus, one of the eyeballs hovered in the aisle, its needle-tail poised over its body, pointing at a chubby boy in a striped shirt.

Just as what had happened outside, everyone suddenly fell silent and seemed to hold a collective breath. Everyone, that was, except for the chubby kid, who whimpered and loudly snuffled snot up his nose.

That was all it took.

The eyeball's needle-tail shot forward into the boy's forehead, piercing him right between the eyes. The thing shuddered, seemed to hesitate a moment and then withdrew its weapon with a wet popping sound.

"Toby!" another boy shrieked as the chubby kid collapsed to the floor, his body twisted at odd angles due to the narrow aisle.

The eyeball swung in the direction of the sound only to be abruptly pummeled with a fat text book swung by the kid who screamed Toby's name.

A thrashing battled ensued and then Natalie was running up the aisle, screaming for everyone to close the windows.

More eyeballs were finding their way inside.

13

Traveling briskly up Main, Ron stopped every person he saw and warned them that demons were headed their way.

He kept repeating the same phrase with every new face he came across: "I saw the eyes...with my own two eyes. Demon eyes! They're coming this way!"

Everyone did their best to ignore him, quickly looking away and moving on before the crazy man did something really scary—like ask them for change.

Ron knew exactly what they were thinking. He would have been thinking the same things that very same morning.

But the world was different now. Just that quick. Hell, HE was different.

"You don't understand," he called after a woman who was hurrying to put distance between herself and him. "This could be the end!"

When she responded by quickening her pace even further, Ron cursed in frustration.

Just get to the police station, he told himself. They'll send a patrol car maybe. See that I'm not lying.

He was about to resume walking again, when a voice came out from inside a car parked at the curb.

"End of the world, huh, man?"

Ron paused, peered at the young guy behind the wheel and then passed him at his companion in the passenger seat—another guy, maybe q few years older than the first.

"I saw them," Ron said cautiously.

"Them?" the first guy questioned.

"They're…eyes. In the field."

"Ah." The driver reached into his shirt pocket and withdrew a crumpled pack of Camels, shaking one out and lighting it with a match while his friend watched Ron with sharp bright eyes. "Eyes. And you think they're demons?"

Ron nodded, uncertain if he should continue this conversation or get his butt moving to the police station. These kids were probably just planning on messing with him anyway.

The passenger spoke up then, leaning forward towards the open window. "How do you know they weren't aliens?"

Frowning, Ron expected both the strangers to laugh uproariously at this joke and then send him on his way with cruel insults about his sanity and intelligence.

But after a beat, he was surprised to find neither of them laughing. In fact, both of the guy's faces remained serious, watching him, waiting for his reaction.

Ron scratched his head. "Aliens?"

The driver nodded and spoke around his cigarette. "Aliens. This is an alien hot-spot, you know."

Shaking his head, Ron conveyed that he did not, in fact, know. "They were eyeballs. I saw them."

"You're assuming aliens will be little green men, right?" the driver asked him, his face still completely serious. "But that may not be the case."

"Truth is," said the passenger. "We have no idea what aliens really look like. What form they might take, to make it either easier for us to comprehend, or if they're hostile, more frightening."

Ron had no idea what these guys were talking about and was no longer interested in finding out. Obviously, they were crazy and had no plans to listen to the truth about the eyeballs.

"Yeah," he said, forcing a smile. "That's cool, guys. But I gotta get to the police station and let them know what's up at the blueberry farm."

Now the passenger laughed. "You never heard of a phone, man?"

The jig was up, Ron knew. They were just toying with the crazy guy. He waved them off and started walking away.

"Hey!"

Ron ignored him, kept moving forward, telling himself he didn't have time to waste on the ignorant.

"Hey! Come back, man. We'll give you a ride."

Stopping, Ron turned back to see the driver poking his head out the window, looking at him earnestly through the haze of cigarette smoke curling up from his mouth.

It only took Ron a moment to consider the offer. Wheels would get him to where he needed to go much faster than his feet could carry him. And what did it matter if they thought he was crazy? Hell, he thought they were crazy.

Unfortunately, it wasn't until he was already in the moving vehicle that the driver said, "We'll drive you to the cops. But first, we want to see the field."

14

Rushing to close the nearest window, Natalie flinched as an eyeball affixed itself to the very glass she was trying to push up, its tiny wing-fins blurred with motion.

Natalie crinkled her nose and wrestled the window up, glancing towards the back of the bus where other kids were racing to close more windows. Unfortunately, it being summer, every single one was cracked at least an inch and there were only twelve of the kids.

Then she remembered Toby sprawled on the aisle floor. Make that eleven.

But she couldn't think about that now. They had to get the rest of these windows closed or else they might all end up like Toby. She didn't know if he was dead or what, but casting a gaze down at his crumpled body, even she could tell it didn't look good. His chubby face had taken on a bluish tinge and white foam was collecting in the corners of his mouth. She tried to determine if his chest was moving, but if it was, it was rising and falling so slowly that it was impossible to detect and Natalie knew she didn't have time to inspect him any closer at the moment.

She also knew that someone should be calling 911 right now, but they were all too busy with the windows. Her own phone was in her bag up front, which was resting in the seat directly behind the driver's.

More shouting caused her to look up, again towards the rear of the bus. The twins, Louie and Mark Marino were doing their best to dodge an eyeball that had found its way inside and was now dive-bombing the two boys as they ducked and hollered.

Stop yelling, Natalie wanted to tell them. They're attracted to the noise!

Instead, she could only watch helplessly as the two brothers did their best, swatting at the eye with their bare hands. Nothing else was available to use as a weapon; the kids hadn't even brought books with them.

Natalie thought again about her backpack up front. Was there anything in there she could use?

The question had barely finished forming in her head when something else caught her eye. Past the other kids and the chaos, outside. Through the windows on the back door of the bus, she could see someone running up the road towards them. A girl, and Natalie thought she recognized her.

Quickly, she stepped over Toby and shoved her way past Louie and Mark, covering her head protectively as she went. By the time she reached the emergency exit in the back, pressing her hands to the dirty glass, she could see quite clearly who was out there, running and waving at them.

It was Lisa, the teenager who lived across the street from Natalie. And Natalie could see by the expression on Lisa's face that she had already spotted the flying eyeballs and the body of O'Brien and that any second now, she would begin to scream.

15

Sweat trickled down the nape of her neck but Lisa barely noticed. She'd dropped her purse a few yards back, but she didn't noticed that either. All she saw was those things, that swarm of things, moving silently through the thick air like some fat nightmare version of dragonflies.

O'Brien was dead—she could see that even from a distance. His face had ballooned to twice its normal size and was a bluish-purple color, wide eyes bulging with surprise in their splitting sockets.

Lisa felt like she couldn't breathe and her belly roiled and rolled like angry thunderheads about to burst. She tried to focus on the back of the bus-could clearly see the kids within it, panicked, frantically trying to close the windows before the eyeballs got in there and did to them what they had done to O'Brien.

A small face appeared in the back window, pale with a halo of wild dark hair, head shaking anxiously, palms pressed flat against the glass.

Realizing who the face belonged to somehow comforted Lisa and she focused solely on Natalie, moving forward without flailing her arms, biting back the scream that had been about to burst from her throat and into the summer sky like a flock of terrified black birds.

Little Natalie. She used to baby sit Natalie not so long ago. She had had to be the grown-up on those nights and she would have to be the grown-up again. Natalie's mother would—

The bus's engine roared to life, cutting off her thoughts. Lisa had to stifle another scream, suddenly sure that she was about to be left behind, here in the middle of nowhere, with those things flying around and her old teacher dead on the ground, already attracting flies and bloating in the late June heat.

16

Travis had closed the windows closest to the front and now his plan was simple: get the hell out of here.

He jumped behind the steering wheel, twisted the key and reached for the gear shift. Instinctively, he checked his side view mirror and that's when he saw her. Even from this far away, he knew his girl-the shape of her, the way she moved.

Lisa was back there, chasing after them. Out in the open, with those deadly eyeballs flying around.

Without hesitation, he threw the bus into reverse and stomped on the gas. Some of the kids shrieked at the sudden jerky movement but as far as he could tell, none of them fell down.

From the back of the bus, he heard Natalie yelling Lisa's name, presumably to him.

"I know!" he shouted back, struggling to be heard over the noisy kids. "Open the emergency door for her!"

Driving the bus in reverse wasn't something Travis was particularly experienced at but he knew he would get them to Lisa faster than she could get to them.

"I can't open it!" Natalie yelled.

Travis dared a glance back and saw her fighting with the safety latch. He cursed under his breath and began shouting at Louie and Mark to get back there and help her. They were both pretty big for their age-especially Louie-and Travis knew they were strong.

Both boys ceased swatting at the eyeball that was buzzing them and hurried to the back, traveling up the aisle drunkenly, grabbing the back of seats to keep their balance.

A moment later Travis was hitting the brakes, stopping just short of where Lisa stood, her arms raised as though warding off impact.

With a sinking feeling of despair, Travis saw that getting hit by a bus was the least of Lisa's worries now.

A huge swarm of eyeballs sailed through the air towards her, stinger tails poised and trembling.

17

The Toyota carrying Ron and his companions shot up the road trailing a thick cloud of dust.

Ron was in the backseat hunkered down low, partly because the car was moving well beyond the speed limit, but also because he had no desire to see those flying eyeballs again once they reached the blueberry fields. He just wanted these two weirdos to see that he wasn't pulling anyone's leg and he wasn't crazy and then they could all be on their way, seeking out help and a solution to get rid of the demonic things.

The passenger, whose name was Nick, was readying a camera in his lap while his buddy Lauran excitedly began talking into a mini voice recorder, relaying their every move since bumping into Ron back on Main.

"What's your name again?" Lauran asked, eyeing Ron in the rearview mirror.

"Ron," Ron said coldly. He was not particularly happy about these guys being so giddy about the whole thing. New age hippies is what he guessed they were. Talking about aliens and all.

"Right," Lauran said, as though he'd been testing Ron to see if he knew the correct answer. Into the recorder, he said, "Ron says they're only slightly bigger than the average blueberry and if that's true—"

"It's true!" Ron snapped.

"If that's true," Lauran went on, ignoring Ron. "Then all the previous data we have on extraterrestrial life is grossly inaccurate."

"Not necessarily," Nick said without looking up.

"Could be that this particular species has never been encountered before."

Lauran made a scoffing sound. "And what are the chances of that?"

Nick simply shrugged, still focused on his camera.

"Slim to none," Lauran answered himself. "In all the history of humankind, it's highly unlikely that no human has yet stumbled across this particular species before."

Ron wondered vaguely why Lauran kept repeating the phrase "this particular species" but decided it was best not to ask. Instead, he said, "No one's encountered them before, believe me."

"And what makes you so sure?" Nick asked.

"Because they're demons, not aliens."

"Demons." Nick sounded skeptical.

"That's right."

"Demons that were made by humans using a new kind of insecticide with the wrong kind of fertilizer."

"Yep."

"That makes no sense at all."

"Makes more sense than damn aliens."

"Says you."

"Right again."

Both men fell silent, giving Lauran a chance to continue talking into his recorder, but not for long.

"There it is!" Ron yelled suddenly, causing the men in the front to jump. He pointed to the field as it came into view. "Right up there!"

Up ahead, the three men saw the yellow school bus and a girl running towards it. Ron squinted, noting that it was the same girl he'd spoken to earlier. He shook his head sadly. "I told her not to come out here but she wouldn't listen."

Lauran dropped his recorder and cursed. "Is that a body?"

"Screw the body," Nick said. "Look at that!"

The Toyota slammed to a stop and the three men watched in wonder as a shifting cloud of eyeballs swarmed the right side of the bus. A silent moment passed and then Nick announced, "We need the camcorder from the trunk."

18

Stepping aside to let the Marino brothers open the emergency door, Natalie spotted the little blue car driving up and skidding to a stop about thirty yards behind the bus. She didn't have time to consider who they might be or what they were doing because in the next instant Louie and Mark got the door open and were hauling Lisa up inside.

Travis was watching from the front and starting shouting for them to close it again, quick. The sentence was barely out of his mouth when he was back behind the steering wheel and the bus was in motion.

Natalie took it upon herself to grab at the swinging emergency door, nearly falling out of the moving bus in the process, but was finally able to get a hold on it and slam it closed. It wasn't until after the door was secure that she noticed Lisa had her around the waist, helping her to keep her balance.

"Thanks," Natalie said as she fell back into one of the seats.

Lisa didn't respond-just whirled away, heading for the front of the bus, casually stepping over Toby, her long dark hair plastered to her sweaty face. She was yelling at Travis and swearing her head off, demanding to know just what "those things" were.

Too busy trying to keep the speeding bus on the road, Travis's answers were short and to the point. "I don't know, but they killed O'Brien."

Natalie felt queasy and her head was beginning to hurt. She couldn't take her eyes off Toby, lying there in the aisle, unmoving, the little hole in his forehead trickling a thread of blood down the bridge of his nose. She studied him for a few ticks of time and then dragged her gaze back up to the rest of her surroundings. Louie Marino was holding his right wrist in his left hand, a pained expression on his face.

"Stung," he said over and over. "Got stung."

Mark was still swatting at one of the eyeballs. He'd taken off his shirt, rolled it up and was whipping it through the air at the creature, too busy to notice his brother until Louie fell to his knees, his eyes swimming out of focus. Mark turned and yelled, the eyeball forgotten as he bent to help his brother.

It was all too much, Natalie thought. They were just kids. How had this happened? And what was this, exactly?

All around her, her classmates were screaming and crying. Very few of them were doing anything about the few eyeballs that had managed to get inside the bus. Most were cowering in their seats, covering their heads with their arms, trying to make themselves invisible.

Natalie couldn't blame them but she also knew hiding wasn't going to help anyone.

Ignoring the pounding in her skull, she slid out of her seat, snatched Mark's T-shirt out of his hand and took over where he had left off.

19

"Where are we going?" Lisa demanded, holding onto the steel bar behind the driver's seat. "We should be going to the police station!"

"School's closer," Travis told her without looking up. His knuckles were white around the steering wheel and Lisa had never seen such a look of intense concentration on his face. Not even when they were... well, not ever.

"Did you call 911?"

"I...no," he admitted. "I didn't think of it. Everything just happened so fast."

Lisa made an unhappy noise and said, "Give me your phone."

Travis shook his head. "I don't want to take my foot off the gas. Those things are following us."

Peering out the window, Lisa saw that he was correct. While most of the swarm was chasing the bus at the rear, a few had picked up enough speed to travel alongside it. "What are those things?" she asked again.

At first, it didn't seem as though Travis was going to reply but a moment later he said, "I think they're... uh...blueberries."

Lisa stared at him. "Blueberries." It was not a question. She didn't know if Travis had skipped a groove or had just picked a really bad time to be joking around.

He shrugged sheepishly. "They came out of the blueberry field, anyway. And look." He let go of the steering wheel just long enough to point to the eyeballs still stuck to the glass in the folding door.

Eyes widening, Lisa studied the creature, paying particular attention to what appeared to be a tiny crown on its "head". Where the berry was attached to the stem, she assumed, if what Travis said was true.

"But…" she started, unsure of how to continue. "How?" she asked finally.

"Hell if I know," Travis said and spun the wheel hard to the right, causing all the kids in the back to fly around. "Sorry," he called, once he'd completed the turn.

"Travis!" Lisa scolded as she held on for dear life. "You're gonna get fired!"

He seemed annoyed by this and snapped, "I thought you were gonna call the police?"

"Give me your phone!"

Travis jerked a thumb backwards. "Get one from them!"

"I have a phone," a voice said and Lisa turned to see Natalie making her way precariously to the front of the bus. In one hand, she was holding out a pink cell phone. In the other, she had what appeared to be a balled up T-shirt.

Lisa gave the girl as much of a smile as she could muster and took the phone, flipping it open and starting to dial.

"Wait," Natalie said. Before Lisa could respond, Natalie was pushing the T-shirt up under her nose. Lisa made a gagging sound and pinched her nose closed with her free hand. She still had a tendency to go into babysitter mode. "Oh, Jeeze, Natalie. Are you sick? Did you throw up?"

"No," Natalie said. "It's one of them. I caught it in the shirt and stomped on it."

The odor assaulted Lisa's sinuses and she sneezed

violently several times. "Get it out of here!" she cried.

Natalie's face fell and Lisa instantly regretted her harshness. She squeezed Natalie's shoulder. "I mean… good job, sweetie."

"I have good aim," the girl said absently and Lisa realized that she was most likely in shock from everything that had happened so far.

"That you do," Lisa agreed.

Nodding at the cell phone, Natalie said, "Remember to tell the cops that."

Puzzled, Lisa asked, "That you have good aim?"

"No. That they'd better have it too."

20

While the girls were having their moment, Travis was mentally cursing up a storm, trying to keep the bus moving fast but not so fast that he flipped the thing, which he knew he was in real danger of doing.

Luckily, the school was only a few blocks away now and as far as he could tell, most of the kids were okay. Except for Toby, of course. And maybe Louie Marino. And whoever else had been tossed around like dice in a cup.

Lisa managed to get Natalie to sit down and was now talking into the pink cell phone. Travis winced when he heard her say the words "mutant blueberries." He suspected that whoever was on the other end of the phone would assume that Lisa was either a complete nutjob or playing a childish prank. Neither option promised a rescue any time soon.

"No, I'm not kidding!" Lisa shouted. "Do I sound like I'm kidding?" There was a pause and then she barked, "Stop laughing! We have kids on this bus!" Another pause and then she was throwing the phone to the floor and screaming, "Man, I hate this town!"

Natalie let out a little cry and jumped up to retrieve her phone. She picked it up, said hello into it several times and made a face. "Laughing," she said.

"Yeah, they think it's a real joke," Lisa replied, plunking herself down on one of the bench seats. Travis said nothing, keeping his eyes on the road, but his heart had sunk to learn they were probably on their own here. He also didn't think he'd ever heard Lisa so angry and that made him even more nervous. He knew she had a bit of a temper and even under mild circumstances had a tendency to be a bit irrational when mad.

Slowing the bus down as he turned onto the school property, he didn't bother with any official parking spot. He pulled the nose of the bus right up to the front door, angling it slightly so that the bus's door was only eight or so feet away.

All at once, the kids flooded forward, some in the depths of catatonia while others were nearly insane with hysteria. Trying to think through all the screaming and crying wasn't easy.

"My brother is dead!" Mark Marino cried, pushing his sweaty shirtless body through the other kids and pounding on the door, completely oblivious to the swarm of flying eyeballs hovering on the other side of the glass. "Let me out!"

Travis could think of no other way to make it into the school beside just barreling through the eyeballs and hoping for the best. He decided it should be himself that lead the way.

He stood and gently moved past the kids and grabbed Mark by the shoulders, pulling him away from the door. Mark went without protest, hugging Travis and pressing his tear-streaked face into the teenager's chest.

Over Mark's head, Travis looked at Lisa. "When I say "go" I want you to open the door. I'll go first, maybe try to distract them if I can. I don't know. You just do whatever you can to get the kids inside."

Lisa offered no protest, just nodded grimly and got into position to swing open the door on Travis's say.

Abruptly, Travis shoved Mark away from him and shouted, "Go!"

The door swung open and he covered his face with a forearm and plunged himself down the steps and into the fray of impossibility.

21

Both Nick and Lauran leapt from the Toyota like two little kids barreling down a staircase on Christmas morning.

Lauran raced over to the dead body and knelt beside it, speaking frantically into his mini-recorder while Nick retrieved their camcorder from the trunk. A moment later he was beside the body as well, camera pointed down, then panning around the vacant blueberry field before coming back to rest on O'Brien.

Still in the car, Ron chewed the skin around his thumb nail, eyes worriedly scanning the fields for any sign of flying eyeballs.

"This sucks," he muttered, watching the two men. If even one eyeball would show itself then they would see that not only was he not crazy, but that the things definitely weren't aliens from space. How could they be? They had started the day as ordinary blueberries. He ought to know. He'd been munching a few of them before all hell had broken loose.

The thought froze his heart.

He'd been eating those things.

The sudden need to vomit was so overwhelming that he didn't even have time to exit the car—just leaned over and puked into the seat beside him.

Even after his stomach was empty, he didn't feel much better. "I'm gonna die," he whispered. The certainty of the statement felt more true than any other words he'd ever spoken and caused him to throw up a second time, his abdomen knotting itself together so tightly that he whimpered in pain.

A shout forced him to straighten up again, to peer bleary-eyed out at the two men he'd just met. Lauran was standing up again, pointing at the field. Or, more aptly, at the swarm above the field. Ron couldn't believe his eyes when the guy actually started to bounce around a little, jumping from one foot to the other the way a little kid will do when they're especially excited.

Lauran wasn't afraid. He was happy.

His alien hunting companion had lowered the camera, watching the swarm slack-jawed. Ron thought that Nick didn't look exactly scared but he didn't look happy either. He seemed more puzzled than anything, as if he was wondering if this could be some kind of joke, or perhaps a hoax.

Just when Ron had thought he'd seen everything, Lauran added to his jumping up and down display by yelling "Yippie!" over and over again.

Ron pounded on the closed window of the car with his fist. "Get back in here," he shouted. "They'll get you!"

Lauran either hadn't heard his warning or was completely ignoring it. Nick on the other hand, glanced back at Ron, his expression alert but confused.

"Come on!" Ron urged. "Hurry!"

To his amazement, Nick suddenly brought the camera up to film him pounding on the glass and shouting.

"What…what are you doing? They're coming! Look behind you!"

Nick, camera to his eye, swung back to face the field and the swarm that was nearly upon him.

The eyeballs attacked Lauran first and his squeals of delight quickly rose in pitch until they were screams of agony. He whirled around, arms flailing, like a man on fire, doing a gruesome death dance that his friend was catching on film. Even after Nick became aware that these were not friendly little ET's, he continued to shoot the footage, capturing Lauran's demise for as long as he dared. An excruciating amount of time later-or so it seemed to Ron, who had fallen silent, tears streaming down his stubbled cheeks-Nick finally turned the camera away and broke into a run for the car, a scream breaking free from deep in his chest as he ran.

That scream was all it took for the eyeballs to turn their attention on him, swooping down, stingers raised and plunging.

Ron watched in helpless horror until it was over and then he waited. He knew the eyeballs would fly back to the field and lay in wait for their next victims. When they did, he planned to exit the car as quietly as possible and search Nick's body for the keys.

And one other thing.

Come hell or high water, he was going to get that camera.

22

Before she'd even registered what she was doing, Natalie had jumped forward and grabbed hold of Travis's belt, tucking her face into his back and using his body as a shield. Together, they bolted for the school's front door as a cloud of eyeballs whirled around them.

Natalie kept her eyes squeezed tightly shut. She didn't want to see those little fin-shaped wings or the red stingers curling up over the tops of their bodies, ready to strike at the first opportunity.

She was surprised that Travis had allowed her to literally tag along, but a moment later she discovered why.

Whoever was behind her and deboarding the bus had taken their cue from her, taking hold of her waistband and moving when she moved, just as she moved when Travis did, everyone carrying a three dimensional, living, breathing shadow on their backs. Even without her eyes open she knew that the rest of her classmates were forming a train being her and that, in all probability, Lisa was acting as the caboose.

She could still hear Mark sniffling but the sound was muffled, as though he was using a hand to cover his mouth. Good thinking, she thought, since these attack blueberries were so drawn to sound.

Travis was moving fast, but not running, and she wanted to tell him to go, go, dammit, go! Was he thinking that she or the rest of the kids wouldn't be able to keep up with him? A ridiculous thought, if true. After all, he was pretty old. Eighteen, she thought. Maybe not as old as her parents but definitely old enough to be slower than a bunch of twelve year olds. If he was holding back on their behalf, then he was probably about to get them all killed with his pokey behavior.

Natalie knew this theory was mostly bogus, just something to keep her mind off what was really happening, but then the truth of the matter thrashed in her fists as Travis began moving in a strange jerky way. He pulled abruptly to the left, making her lose her grip on his belt and instinctively open her eyes.

What she saw caused her breath to clot in her throat: Travis was smacking at the creatures with his bare hands, his eyes wild and whirling in their sockets. As Natalie and the others watched, he began to speak in a loud commanding voice.

"Get inside," he told them all. Any eyeballs that weren't on him already took notice of him then, swinging his way with menacing purpose. "If I keep talking, they won't notice you." He hissed in pain and gritted his teeth as one of the stingers sunk deep into the meaty heel of his hand. "Go!"

Natalie hesitated only a moment, started for the school's front doors, but then turned back when a piercing wail froze her in place.

It was Lisa, who'd rushed over to join Travis in his losing battle, first to try dragging him away, but quickly assessing the situation for herself. She let out a bloodcurdling scream of defiance before seeming to break into enthusiastic applause.

Stunned, it took Natalie a moment to realize that Lisa was actually catching eyeballs between her hands and crushing them, clapping them out of the air the way people do when they see a pesky fruit fly hovering above their dinner plate.

The other kids weren't nearly as impressed by the show of sacrifice and practically bowled Natalie over on their way to the front door. But Natalie stood transfixed, watching with increasing dread as tears began to roll down Travis's face and him lips began to move, though produced no sound. Sweating and flushed with pain, he sank to his knees, his eyes meeting hers one last time. Natalie clearly saw the pleading there and to her complete amazement, Travis smiled. A small, weak smile that was mostly obscured by all the eyeballs fluttering around him, but a smile none the less.

Natalie forced herself to smile back, glancing quickly at Lisa who'd begun to howl in agony as not one, but two, stingers pierced her left eye.

Seeing all she wanted to see, Natalie turned and fled for safety.

23

It took him ten minutes of slowly crawling on his belly like a soldier, but Ron finally reached the video camera and gripped it in one badly trembling hand.

He did his best not to look at the three bodies curled on the ground, keeping his mind focused on the task of moving as silently as possible.

Finding Nick's car keys proved to be much less of a challenge than he'd thought it would be: they were lying next to the alien hunter's body, probably had still been in his hand when he'd been attacked.

Ron said a silent prayer thanking God for this favor. He also mentally gave the blueberry field a stout middle finger, telling those tiny demons just what they could do with their deadly little stingers.

He tried not to think about the fact that he'd eaten some of them this morning, or what they could mean to his health—both physical and mental-when this was over.

If it was ever over.

He just hoped it didn't mean he was damned.

Crawling back the way he'd come, he was pretty sure that God wouldn't hold it against him. He hadn't read the bible in many years, but he couldn't recall any passage that said it was a sin to eat demons, particularly if it had been accidental. He figured he fairly was safe in that regard. But he made a mental note to ask forgiveness for it just the same, just in case.

Impatience made him crawl back to the car faster

than he'd crawled away from it and he made it to the Toyota in half the time, clambering inside, tossing the camera onto the passenger seat and closing the door as quietly as possible.

It wasn't until he started the engine that it occurred to him to wonder what happened to the bus. It was gone and the people with it.

He couldn't ponder it for long though. The sound of the engine had brought the little Hell beasts back, whizzing towards him like angry blue bumblebees.

With a squeak of fright, Ron stomped on the accelerator and the little car shot forward, fishtailing for several seconds until he gained control. He paid no mind to where he was going—as long as it was away from that field. Luckily, he didn't have to give it much thought as the road only went in one direction: straight.

Checking the rearview mirror, he saw that the little buggers could speed along at a nice clip when they wanted to and he groaned miserably. Would this day never end?

Ron floored the car, his jaw set with grim determination as he debated on turning around and trying yet again to go for help. For the moment at least, he had a little bit of a lead on the flying eyeballs and the thought of reversing direction and driving headlong into them made his stomach kick again.

No, he had to go forward.

Wracking his brain, he thought about what was up ahead. Nothing he could think of that would provide a safe haven, except for maybe the school.

He blinked in surprise.

The school. Of course! That's where the kids had gone. There would be phones there, not to mention it was a good solid brick structure. If he could just get inside without getting killed, then there was no way those demon eyes could follow.

For the first time since this whole bizarre incident began, Ron felt a twinge of hope for his future.

24

Standing at the glassed front door looking out, Natalie wept freely at the collapsed bodies of her former baby sitter and the cute bus driver. As she did, a few stray eyeballs ticked against the glass, searching for a way in. In an act of defiance, she flipped them off one by one, knowing that the gesture was one she surely would be grounded for if her parents had seen her doing it. But, she thought, maybe they would have cut her some slack this time, given the circumstances.

The other kids had all disappeared, though she wasn't sure where to. Calling their parents, most likely, or looking for an adult somewhere. She was about to turn away from the door herself when she saw a car racing towards the front of the school. It was the same car she'd seen at the blueberry field.

Natalie knew she should feel happy knowing that a grown-up had to be driving that car, but she couldn't help feeling a sense of unease when she saw that it was being chased by yet another swarm of flying eyeballs. She debated on locking the door—the driver would probably be okay if he just stayed inside his car until help arrived. But in the end, she knew she couldn't do that. Inside the school would certainly be safer than out there, car or not.

In the end though, it wouldn't have mattered if she'd locked it, as she soon discovered. With growing alarm, she watched the little car approach, weaving more and more the closer it got to the school, until it was driving up first one curb and then the opposite curb in a space of seconds.

Shouting a word she knew she would have been grounded for-attacking eyeballs or not-Natalie leapt out of the way as soon as the Toyota bumped up the sidewalk in front of the school, clipped the side of the bus and aimed itself straight at her.

The car crashed through the wide doors with a deafening screech of tires and metal and glass crunching against each other before slamming to a halt a mere ten feet from where Natalie had rolled across the floor.

Someone was screaming.

Confused, Natalie sat up, coughing, waving dust out of her face as she struggled to see inside the car. Before she could determine what was happening with the driver however, she was distracted by the swarm of eyeballs flowing into the school by the dozen.

Natalie groaned aloud, then clapped a hand over her mouth to silence herself.

This was it then.

They were all screwed.

A man fell out of the car and Natalie recognized him as the field hand she'd spoken to this morning, the one who'd taken off running the moment he realized the blueberries had turned to eyeballs.

She scowled. Why had he come back, if he was such a coward? Not to mention, he'd brought the things with him.

The guy rolled around on the floor, blood dribbling from a shallow cut on his forehead. He was wiping at his eyes, obviously trying to clear his vision.

Natalie knew when he was able to see again because that's when he shut up, his gaze focused on the eyeballs heading his way.

This is so messed up, she thought and began

crawling towards him. Her intention was to whisper in his ear: be quiet! If they could just move silently, she hoped they might make it to the school gymnasium where they could barricade themselves until help arrived. After all, it was the gym people came to during flooding season. It must be safe.

But the field hand didn't wait for her to reach him.

He rose to his feet in slow motion and began backing away from the destroyed Toyota, his eyes fixed on the tiny terrors swooping all around him. Listening, Natalie knew. The things were listening.

She followed his lead, standing up as quietly as possible and moving down the hall, being careful to avoid stepping on any broken glass or twisted metal that happened to be in her path.

The man stopped when he saw her, his eyes widening and much to her surprise, he raised a video camera, pointing it directly at her for several seconds before twisting around to shoot the flying eyeballs.

Natalie froze in place. Her brain was becoming overloaded with all the weirdness and why a field hand with a video camera should be the final straw for her, she didn't know but there it was. She felt ready to snap.

When the man looked at her again, she saw his own eyes burning with insanity and for whatever reason, that sight was enough to get her moving again.

She pointed towards the rear of the school, silently telling him that that was the direction they needed to go in.

He seemed to understand, nodding slowly.

Then the silence shattered when he suddenly let out a surprised cry of pain. He and Natalie looked down simultaneously to see one of the little eyeballs plunging it's stinger into his knee. Natalie had time to wonder if the thing was just merely curious but the cry was enough to get the attention of all the others and the next thing she knew, the field hand was running down the hall at full speed.

This is it, she thought, taking off after him. Do or die.

25

Ron couldn't believe how fast the little girl could run. She was easily keeping pace with him and he had the feeling that she wasn't even running as fast as she could.

Behind them, the eyeballs gave chase.

"We have to get to the gym," the girl said, barely panting. "We take a right at the end of the hall."

He wanted to ask why but he didn't have the breath or the inclination. All he wanted was away from those little hellacious beasts and he was willing to put his trust in a child to get him there.

The girl pulled ahead, and then abruptly skidded to a stop. Ron nearly rear-ended her but weaved at the last possible second.

When he saw what she had stopped to look at, he stopped himself, just a few feet past her.

Together they stood outside the cafeteria where a bunch of kids were sitting at tables, casually eating lunch.

At their arrival, a few of the children glanced over without much interest. Ron frowned, the situation perhaps the most surreal of the whole day, but when he glanced back the way he and the girl had just come, he saw the swarm still after them, moving much slower, almost lazily, but definitely still on their way.

The girl grabbed his wrist and pulled him forward into the cafeteria.

"Come on," she said, racing by the tables, ignoring the other kids, Ron in tow. "There's a phone in the kitchen."

She pushed her way through a swinging door and then they were in a sterling environment, ovens, freezers, counters all gleaming bright silver.

Skittering around the huge appliances, they both stopped short yet again when they saw the cafeteria cook dressed in white and stirring something in a huge silver bowl. He looked up from his task with irritation.

"Did you bring them?" the cook asked.

Both Natalie and Ron blinked at the man.

"What?" Natalie asked.

"The blueberries," he snapped impatiently. Then his gray eyes moved past them and his scowl deepened. "Oh, come on! Why did you have to do that? You think this is funny?"

"Huh?" Ron had no idea why this guy was so angry. Had the entire world turned inside out or what? "What's funny?"

The cook moved away from his counter and his shiny silver bowl, pointing with a pudgy finger to the floor behind where Natalie and Ron stood. In unison, they both turned to see blueberries scattered all over the linoleum. Hundreds of them, just laying there as though spilled from a basket.

Ron worked his jaw but no sound came out. He felt close to passing out and placed a hand on a refrigerator to steady himself.

The blueberries were perfectly ordinary. Some riper than others, but except for that, quite perfect: fat and blue and ready for munching.

Natalie sank to the floor, bringing her knees up to her chin and hugging them tightly. Slowly, she began to rock back and forth, her eyes going vacant.

Looking down at the camera in his hand, Ron realized that he had the proof right there. The whole day hadn't been some bizarre dream. He could show them.

But when he tried to play back the tape, there was no visual beyond static. The audio was fine. Screams had been recorded aplenty, but of course that was nothing more than jokesters having a good time, hollering away like they were in a spooky Halloween movie. At least, that's what everyone else heard when they listened to it in the coming days.

"Who's gonna help me pick all those up?" the cook growled at them. "Do you want blueberry cobbler for dessert or not?"

Ron didn't stay to listen anymore. He fled from the cafeteria and out of the school, passing the crashed car on his way out.

The bodies of the two teenagers were gone.

Feeling like a man in a Dali nightmare, Ron ran all the way back to the field to find the bodies of the alien hunters also gone. As if they had never existed.

And when he thought about it, who had known them anyway, beside himself? Probably no one.

And the teenagers? Most likely ran off together, the way teenagers sometimes do. Maybe they'd be back someday. Maybe not.

Ron suspected not.

He stood, panting, staring out at the blueberry fields, sweat rolling down his back and staining the armpits of his work shirt. Rooted to the ground, he didn't move for a very long time. He was waiting. Waiting to see what would happen next. But nothing ever did.

SMIRK

Paul was in the grocery store shopping for cleaning supplies on a bright Thursday morning in April when he saw the woman with the shocking blue eyes and blonde hair that fell to her shoulders in a cascade of yellow waves. She, like him, was browsing, her pushcart full of vegetables and fruits, healthy cereal and soy milk.

He was instantly drawn to her. She clearly had the priority of her health in order, same as him, and she was gorgeous. She must have been around 5'9", tall for a woman, late twenties, maybe, and quite thin, perhaps a bit too thin. Paul suspected she might go a little too hard on the cardio, which a lot of women did. They certainly loved their treadmills.

Watching her out of the corner of his eye, he pretended to be scrutinizing a Windex label, quickly turning away when she glanced in his direction, but looking back again just as quickly a second later.

She carefully placed an eco-friendly cleanser in her cart and started off down the aisle, pausing again to consider sponges. This afforded him a spectacular view of her heart-shaped, tight ass, clad in snug gray yoga pants. Usually Paul would scoff in disgust at any woman wearing work-out clothes in public but this one pulled it off gloriously.

When she turned the corner of the aisle and disappeared from sight, Paul decided to follow. Casually, of course. No need to be a creep about it. He started after her at a leisurely pace after dumping the window cleaner into the small red basket he carried.

He found her again, browsing paperback novels this time, and he slowed down as he passed by, curious as to which kind of fiction she was most interested in. Currently she was reading the back cover copy of a Dean Koontz novel. He frowned slightly, preferring something by

David Baldacci himself. Maybe John Grisham. Novels with some meat on them rather than supernatural fluff written in a week's time. He felt a sense of satisfaction when she put the Koontz back and reached for Janet Evanovich instead. Also not his choice but at least more appropriate for the kind of woman she seemed to be. The independent sort, he imagined.

He also took the opportunity to check her left hand for a wedding band and smiled a bit when he saw she wasn't wearing one. No jewelry at all in fact. Another good sign. She wasn't vain or superficial.

Pausing at the magazines, Paul made a bit of a show in choosing which fitness mag he was interested in, hoping she would notice his perusing of Men's Heath. In truth, he already had this same copy at home on his nightstand. If she happened to visit his bedroom in the near future, he'd have to either flip it over or hope she wasn't that observant. He assumed it would be the latter though. Most women were far too self-involved to notice small details like magazine covers, especially given what he imagined the circumstances would be in the event she was in his room.

He smiled a little, turning his face away from her for the briefest of seconds, lest she think he was gay and happy about leafing through a magazine featuring shirtless buff dudes. He had a quick vision of himself as regulated to the friend zone, her thinking of him as one of the girls, and inwardly shuddered at the thought. Paul cleared his throat and put the magazine back on the shelf quickly, his eyes frantically scanning for something more fitting. The noise caused her to glance at him and he saw her eyes swiftly travel from his face, down his body and back up again.

Was that satisfaction her saw in her gaze? Appreciation? Lust?

He lifted one corner of his mouth, a careful, noncommittal smile. She gave him the same smile in return. It lasted maybe half a second before she looked away, back to the book in her hand.

He wondered if it was good or bad that she had withdrawn her attention so quickly. Maybe she was shy. Or being coy. Certainly she must have enjoyed the sight of him. Nearly all women did. In addition to being in peak physical condition-something he displayed by wearing T-shits at least two sized too small and tight jeans-he also had an exceptionally handsome face. Some women had even gone so far as to tell him he was "movie star handsome," which he neither agreed nor disagreed. It depended on the movie star. He was more Ryan Gosling, for instance, than Mel Gibson. He had sandy-blond hair, cut fashionably, but it was often said that his eyes were his most arresting feature: light green with darker green striations shot through. Not to mention his smile. His smile, he knew, could stop hearts. He'd been told that before too. All in all, he'd been blessed not only with phenomenal genes but also the willingness and the drive to keep himself in top shape and only put the very best foods in his body.

The woman was moving away again, which he was proud he'd noticed at all, given how lost in his own thoughts he'd become.

He waited a few heartbeats before following behind her.

She turned her head, casting a brief glance over her shoulder. So, she knew he was trailing her. He suspected that by now she knew he was interested and imagined that inside, she was giggling like a school girl. He was impressed with her ability to contain herself. Flattery often made women blush uncontrollably, but she was a cool customer. He liked it.

Next, she made her way past the meat department and he was mildly distressed when she didn't stop. He didn't eat much meat, and only chose the leanest possibilities when he did, but he knew not eating meat at all was a sign of weakness. Usually vegetarians and, even worse, vegans, more often than not held animals in a ridiculously high regard, insisting they were on the same evolutionary scale as humans, which was simply not true. Animals had been put on earth for the use and convenience of people. It was a raw deal for them, without a doubt, but it was the truth. Anyone who let that fact keep them awake at night needed to take a long, hard look at their lives and reevaluate some things.

However, maybe the woman already had a freezer full of meat and he was off on a tangent, worrying for nothing.

He put the thought out of his head and focused instead on the gentle sway of her hips as she pushed her cart along, heading towards the front of the store.

Realizing she was probably on her way to checkout, he knew he had to make his move now or perhaps regret not doing so forever.

He increased his pace, pushing his own cart up alongside hers. She looked at him and it was time for his ace in the hole: he grinned.

To his amazement, her expression didn't change whatsoever.

Okay, then. Super shy or a very cool customer. He wasn't used to a non-reaction but he could work with it. He'd always enjoyed a challenge.

"I saw you back there looking at books," he said, still smiling. "Nice to know there's still a few people left in the world who enjoy reading."

Her pretty brow furrowed the tiniest bit.

"Anyway," he ventured on, "I noticed you noticing me too."

Nothing. Absolutely nothing. His smile, he knew, was beginning to show the first signs of wavering. He reached out, putting a hand on her cart, stopping it as well as his own. He stuck out his right hand. "I'm Scott."

Her expression flittered and Scott, for one horrifying moment, he thought he saw a flash of anger in her eyes. Then it was gone and her face was neutral again.

"Scott," she said.

"Yep. What's your name?"

The furrow in her brow deepened. She hesitated, the replied, "Hailey. Look, is there something I can help you with?"

The question took him off guard. "Excuse me?"

"You've been following me around and I wondered if maybe we'd been in a class together or something, but..." She trailed off, waiting for an explanation.

He grinned again. "Are you being serious right now?

She looked at him blankly.

"You seriously expect me to believe you don't know what's going on? I've heard of women playing hard to get, but wow. You are good!"

"I beg your pardon?"

"Come on. I was checking you out. You were checking me out. Neither one of us are married. We should get together for a drink sometime. That's it. No big mystery."

Realization dawned on her face and, much to her credit, Scott thought it looked almost genuine.

"Oh. You're using a line. Trying to pick me up."

He laughed, expecting her to do the same, but she didn't.

"How about this," she said. "How about, no."

He blinked. "No?"

"Thanks but no thanks."

Staring at her, he wondered if she was joking. She must be, right?

Then she gave him the same look as she had upon first seeing him-the up and down scanning-and began to turn away. But in the instant before he would be looking at the back of her head, he saw it and it was unmistakable, undeniable.

She smirked.

She smirked and he knew exactly what it meant. He hadn't ever dealt with it himself, but he'd seen it directed towards other men in the past. He recognized it.

It was a smirk that said, I'm too good for you. You are not even on the same planet as me, never mind in the same ballpark. You are so far beneath me, you're barely a speck in my vision. Less than a dust mote. You are literally nothing.

The understanding was nothing short of shocking. Scott stood rooted to the glossy linoleum floor, other customers moving around him, as he watched her go. He felt dazed, as though he'd suffered a hard blow to the head. Part of his mind didn't want to believe it and he probably wouldn't have if not for that goddamn smirk. That self-satisfied, self-righteous fucking smirk.

And just like that, his shock was ignited into fury. He abandoned his shopping cart, heading straight for the automatic doors, through them and out into the hard September sunshine. He walked past the dozens of newly piled pumpkins, past the plant and flower displays and then stopped, his back against the tan brick building, out of sight for the most part, with a perfect view of the grocery store's exit.

He didn't have to wait long. Hailey emerged about five minutes later. She carried two plastic grocery sacks, one in each hand, and strode with purpose through the parking lot. She eventually stopped in the middle of it, at a light blue Prius, which beeped before she dropped her purchases into the back.

Scott was already walking briskly towards her, paying no mind to any cars which may have been travelling through the lot.

Hailey moved around to the driver's side just as Scott was coming up, rounding the back of the car. Glancing around, she saw him an instant before his fist smashed hard into her face. The cartilage in her nose made an audible crunch as she stumbled back, gripping the edge of the open car door with one hand, which was the only thing that kept her in an upright position.

Quickly glancing around, Scott saw that not a single soul was paying attention to them. Most people were either too busy herding children, loading their cars or staring down at their phones.

Good.

He grabbed the stunned and bleeding woman by the throat, twisted her body around and shoved her into the driver's seat while simultaneously snatching the car keys from the ground where she'd dropped them.

"Move over," he said, all evidence of affability evaporated.

"Huh?" Hailey brought a hand to her face with a grimace, took it away to find it streaked with blood. "What…?"

"Move to the passenger seat or I'll bash your face in against the steering wheel.

Clearly confused, Hailey was just starting to realize

what had happened. She opened her mouth, maybe to attempt a scream, which Scott preemptively prevented by grabbing a fistful of her pretty blonde hair and thrashing her head violently. He heard her neck crack and she cried out in pain.

"One more time," he said, aware that a young man in a pickup truck was slowly cruising by and gazing at them with mild interest. "Move the fuck over."

Finally Hailey did as she was told and Scott slipped into the driver's seat, slamming the door door fast.

"If you try to jump out, I'll run you the fuck over."

Hailey said nothing but tears began to trickle down her cheeks.

"You believe me?" he asked.

She nodded slowly.

He locked all the doors and windows from the electrical panel set into the driver's side door.

He had no idea what he was doing, had never done anything like it before, but he was happy for it now. This stuck-up bitch wasn't smirking now, was she? Fuck, no. He was doing all of mankind a favor. A small one, sure, but because of his actions today, there would be one less woman in the world who thought she was better than men.

"Give me your driver's license," he said.

"What?" She sniffed. "Why?"

"Because I told you to."

"But-"

"This is how it's gonna work," he told her. "You are going to do exactly what I say without question. Why? Because if you don't, I'm going to hurt you very badly. I'll probably scar you. No plastic surgery will ever erase what I'll do to you. Do you understand?"

Crying harder, she nodded.

"Now hand over the license."

With shaking hands, she reached for a small purse tucked into a compartment in the center console but Scott suddenly suspected she might have some sort of weapon hidden within and snatched it up before her hands made contact with it. He rifled through the contents until he came up with a wallet and found the license, eyeing the address.

"You still live here?"

She nodded.

"Alone?"

"I…yes."

"Why the hesitation?"

She said nothing, her eyes frightened.

"Do you want me to hurt you?"

Quickly, she shook her head.

"Who do you live with?"

"Just a cat."

"A cat? That's it?"

She nodded. "Charlie."

"The cat's name is Charlie?"

"Yes." She began to sob, long, hitching breathes shaking her entire body. "You're not…not…going to hurt…him, are you?"

"Hurt the cat? Why the fuck would I do that? He never did anything wrong. Unless he's a cold fucking bitch like you. But if he's male…" He trailed off before adding, "I have nothing against animals."

Scott started the engine. The Prius was a little odd to drive, as quiet as it was, but he found it immediately soothing, pulling out of the parking lot without incident and merging smoothly with traffic, driving north through town.

"Where are you taking me?" She asked between sniffles. Her eyes were already developing two very impressive purple-black shiners and he couldn't help but feel a tinge of pride at what he'd accomplished so far.

"You're not too bright, are you?" he said, not bothering to hide the amusement in his voice. "I'm taking you home, stupid."

"Home?" She sounded incredulous. "My home? But...but why not your home?"

"Well." He thought about it. "It's not like I planned this and since I don't know what's going to happen between us, I'd rather have my DNA all over your house than yours over mine. From what I've seen on TV, I think this is the smartest move. My DNA isn't in any files but yours sure as shit will be."

Scott didn't know if Hailey was following his logic but she did start to cry harder still. He glanced at her. "Who's smirking now, huh, your fucking highness?" He let that sink in for a second before continuing. "Besides, my place is immaculate and I'd like it to stay that way. No offense to you, of course. You might be a tidy person yourself but still...I'm probably tidier."

She made no reply, not that he'd expected her to. They drove on in silence interrupted only occasionally by him asking things like left or right. He had a general idea of where her neighborhood was and didn't require much help in getting them there.

Her house was quite lovely, a small yellow bungalow style with green trim, set off the road atop a little hill, trees flanking either side, beds of flowers in the front offset with tall hedges hugging the front facing walls.

Scott pulled the car into an unattached single occupancy garage, the electronic door opener found in the same center console compartment as her tiny purse, closing the door behind them once they were inside.

They sat still, neither moving for a long moment until he said, "I bet you're sorry you gave me that snotty stuck-up smile now."

"I didn't—" she began to protest but Scott put an end to that with a hard backhand to her face. Not too hard, not hard enough to hurt himself-he definitely could have gone harder-but with just enough force to shut her up and let her know he wasn't going to tolerate any lies.

She cried out, raising a hand to protect her face from further blows.

"Shall we go inside?" he suggested pleasantly. He was enjoying himself quite a bit and couldn't wait to continue his fun in a more roomy atmosphere.

"What are you going to do to me?"

He shrugged, honestly unsure. "Maybe we'll just talk. I'd really be interested in knowing how you got to be such a raging cunt. Daddy issues?"

She ignored the question, uttering only one word: "Talk."

It wasn't a question and he supposed that was an improvement.

"No surprises in there for me?" he asked.

"No."

"Promise?"

"Well…just Charlie."

Good Christ. Back to the damn cat again. "Okay, let's go. And remember, if you do anything, try to run away-anything-I will hurt you in ways you never thought possible." He studied her face, focusing on her eyes, which remained terrified, giving him an intense amount of satisfaction. "Do you understand?"

Docile, she nodded.

As they both got out of the car and exited the garage through a side door, Scott marveled at how easy it had all been. It was no wonder women were always getting themselves killed. They'd never admit it but when push came to shove, they were absolutely petrified of even minor violence perpetrated against them. Men were used to it-not coddled like newborn kittens for their entire lives. This idea was something he wanted to ponder further once he finished here. Read up on the subject. Perhaps write his own missive about it. He knew now that he had something to contribute to the topic of the battle between the sexes.

At the front door, he handed Hailey the keys so as not to be seen fumbling with them by a passerby. Also, he knew it was smarter to keep her in front of himself rather than behind where she might get it into her head to flee.

The previously sunny day was rapidly cooling down and becoming overcast with heavy, gray clouds, and when he and Hailey stepped into the house, it was far darker than he'd expected.

Closes the door behind him, he said, "Turn on a light."

She did as commanded and Scott found himself in a pleasant enough kitchen. Small, and as he'd guessed, not as neat as his own, but passable. There were too many things on the countertop, for instance. Bills and other mail, a catalog, a balled up dish towel next to the dish-rack. All things she could easily had found more appropriate places for had she put in even a minute amount of effort.

Glancing into the sink he saw a coffee mug, rinsed out, but still not put away for some mysterious reason. Had she been in such a hurry to get to the grocery store that she'd been unable to complete such a simple task?

He sighed and looked at her. "Well. Here we are."

"What do you want?"

Now that he was inside, with no worry of witnesses, he really thought about the question. "You know," he began. "What I'd really want is a time machine. We could go back to those moments in the store and you could be kind to me. Show some gratitude for my attention. Be flattered."

She swallowed and he noticed her fists clenching and unclenching at her sides.

"No?" he asked. "That's not what you'd want? You're perfecting happy with your rude behavior?"

"I wasn't rude," she said.

He had to laugh at that. "Oh, well, that figures. You're so used to everyone treating you like a princess you just assume that's the way of the world. So…let this be a wakeup call. The world does not revolve around you. You're not even very hot, now that I'm getting a better look at you. Maybe a five, at best. I mean, sure, you have a sweet ass but your personality just ruins it. No one likes a stuck up bitch, Hailey."

She regarded him stonily and he had to wonder if her fear was subsiding. Too much talking, perhaps but whatever reason, he didn't like it. Not at all.

"Pulling a bit of attitude now?" he asked. When she didn't reply, he decided to up the ante. "Where's the bedroom?

She remained silent. Definitely getting too comfortable with the situation.

Scott slammed the side of his fist onto the counter, causing things to rattle, but Hailey's flinch was nearly nonexistent and therefore unsatisfying.

"Where's the fucking bedroom?" he roared, raising the fist threateningly.

She lifted an arm and pointed. "There's one down the hall but that's mainly my office."

81

Scott could feel the blood pounding in his temples. "Where's the fucking bed? Where do you sleep?"

"In the basement. I remodeled it when I bought the place two years ago. Much cooler in the summer. I sleep and workout down there."

"Good. Was that so hard?"

"No."

He resisted the urge to smile at her. "Okay. Lead the way."

Without hesitation, Hailey moved by him and started down a hallway off the kitchen. "It's this way."

He couldn't believe the change in her demeanor. As if she no longer cared what happened to her. She was in shock, he supposed. He'd heard it could really mess with a person.

As he followed her down the long dark hall, he wondered where the cat was. Maybe it was an outdoor cat part of the time and she'd let it out earlier? Maybe it was old and deaf and didn't hear them come in? Or, and Scott thought this the most likely, the cat knew was a smirking, stuck up cunt his owner was and simply couldn't be bothered to greet her. Probably dreaded seeing her at all. Scott knew if he'd been in old Charlie's position, he would have run away long ago, but only after clawing and destroying anything he could get his little paws on.

He put the cat out of his mind when they reached the basement door and Hailey opened it. She flicked a switch, illuminating a fine staircase covered in light blue carpet.

"Down here," she said.

He gestured that she was to descend first.

"Afraid I'll shove you down?" she asked, peering at him over her shoulder.

Scott bristled, feeling his ears and cheeks burn. He

forced a smirk onto his face, knowing she'd appreciate the value of it. "Guess I'll have to rape your fucking asshole for even thinking that, cunt. Now, go!"

She went, leaving him wondering why he'd said such a thing. He'd never spoken anything so vile to a woman before. Yes, he'd thought similar things before-every man had, and if they said otherwise, they were pussy, white-knight liars-but actually threatening a woman with sexual violence was something else all together. Later, he'd have to have a good long think about how he'd been provoked to such an extreme degree.

Hailey, for her part, didn't react to the threat in any way. She simply started down the stairs into the well-lit basement below. Scott followed close behind, close enough that he could grab a fistful of her hair if need be. He was tempted to do it just for the hell of it. Maybe give her a shove. See who the wiseass was when she was laying at the bottom with a goddamn broken arm, or worse. The thought of 'or worse' was quite pleasing, actually.

Again, he resisted his most primal desire and followed her down without so much as breathing on her. He felt a twinge of pride at his self control. He doubted any other man could have managed it.

When they reached the bottom, he immediately saw two other doors off the main room. "What's through there?"

"Laundry room and bathroom," she replied, her voice dull. She was resigned, he realized. Even though he wasn't sure himself what he was going to do, Hailey knew that whatever he chose was inevitable.

Finally he allowed himself to smile at her. "Who's smirking now?"

In a blur of motion, Hailey kicked out, nailing him

hard in the crotch. The pain was so exquisite that it didn't register with his brain immediately. Instead, he felt an intense wave of nausea that doubled him over at the waist, allowing her to bring up a knee which connected excruciatingly first with the bridge of his nose and then again with his mouth.

He would have screamed if he'd had the breath. Hitting the floor, he was only able to make a pathetic squeaking sound, one hand instinctively moving to protect his already swelling balls while the other reached up to his ruined lips. He was dimly aware of a flat dripping sound-fluid muffled as it sank into the carpet.

Through watering eyes, he looked up just as the sole of a shoe crashed into his face. He wished he would lose consciousness after the first stomp, but he didn't. He wasn't quite that lucky.

***

When he came to, the first thing he was aware of was agony. His tongue felt strange in his mouth and when he tried to lick his lips, sharp, jagged edges assaulted it. All of his front teeth-both top and bottom-were shattered. His heart lamed hard, panic overcame him, but he found he could only just barely open one eye and all of his limbs were immobilized. His head throbbed and his stomach churned.

Some terrible, terrible accident.

Must be.

Worse than a car wreck. An explosion?

"Welcome back," a female voice said.

A nurse?

"As you said before," the woman continued. "Who's smirking now?"

Everything came crashing back to him then. The stuck up bitch. He had wanted to punish her somehow, teach her a lesson. About manners, about how to take a compliment from a man, especially when he was under no obligation to offer the compliment in the first place. When he could have any woman he wanted and he picked her out of a crowd.

The fucking ungrateful, snotty cunt.

Even over the pain in his body, his rage burned fiercely."What the fuck did you do?" He tried to snarl the words but even to his own ears, they sounded muddled and slurred, barely understandable.

"What the fuck did I do?" She sounded amused. She moved into his tiny frame of vision, a blurred face, only identifiable by blonde hair. "What would you do, Scott? You followed me around the grocery store, thinking you're king shit of turd mountain and apparently you don't take rejection with even the smallest amount of grace. You stalked, assaulted me, kidnapped me and threatened to rape me. So, I ask again, what would you do?"

He didn't like the question. "Fuck you, cunt."

There was a long pause which gave him a bit of satisfaction. It meant she was off-balance. Probably not used to being called a cunt. Didn't know how to react. Always treated like a fucking queen.

She sighed and moved out of his line of sight. A moment later she spoke, her voice somewhere off to his left and behind him.

"Okay," she said. "I'll tell you what I did, but bear in mind that it's really you who did it to yourself."

Scot coughed, tasting blood, and she politely waited for him to finish before continuing.

"In short," she said. "I kicked your ass. I have to admit I was surprised by your attack in the parking lot but you might be even more surprised that I've taken more than a few self-defense courses. That never occurred to you, did it? That I might, if given a chance, be able to defend myself, particularly in a one-on-one situation. So, that's what I did." She paused for a few seconds and Scott could sense her pacing back and forth.

"I could have let you drive me anywhere but I saw an opportunity and I took it. Just like you did. I brought you to my house, not because I was terrified of you-though I have to admit it was nerve wracking-but because I wanted to get you alone. Like I said, one-on-one. I had to assume you didn't have an actual weapon, given the circumstances of where we...uh... met...how you were dressed and the fact that you neither used one or displayed one. You were counting on intimidation and brute force to be your weapons."

She appeared in front of him again.

"That was your biggest mistake," she went on. "Over-confidence in your own abilities and under-estimating your opponent. Not a good combination. As you are now discovering."

Scott wanted to scream but he refused to give her the satisfaction. Instead, he struggled against his restraints, trying to free his arms. They were both tightly, painfully, fastened to the arms of a chair.

"Oh, you're not going anywhere," she said. "That chair you're in may feel comfortable enough on your ass but it came from my father's restaurant. The only soft thing is the cushion. The rest is fully welded sixteen-gauge steel. You might think you're a tough guy but you're staying put until I let you go. Oh, and in case you're wondering why you don't feel any rope burns on your wrists? It's because you're not bound with ropes of any kind. I used all my old bikes locks.

Three of them. That's braided steel with a nice ABS coating that'll protect your tender baby skin. One around your ankles, another around your wrists and the last one, around your neck, is also wound around a concrete support post. So, yeah, you'll be staying here a while."

His heart, which had barely slowed its frantic thumping, began slamming at full throttle again. He tried to thrust his head forward and was rewarded with only a small fraction of movement before he was choked by the restraint. He coughed and gagged, immediately relaxing his neck.

"Told you," she said. "By the way, all the locks are combination locks. Even if you could see them and get your hands free, you'd have about a one in ten thousand chance of guessing the correct combo. Times two, I suppose."

"Let me go," he croaked.

"No."

He was shocked at the strength in her voice but knew at this point, nothing should shock him. She was clearly out of her mind.

"You're gonna go to prison for this," he said, his voice still sounding like his face was pressed into a pillow.

"Maybe," she agreed, unconcerned. "But, if I do, while I'm sitting there rotting away, I'll take all the comfort and solace I can by thinking about you and these moments, as well as all the future moments we're going to share."

"You fucking crazy bitch! I'll—"

She punched him in his already agonized mouth. "What does that make you then?" she demanded, leaning forward in his face while he groaned, blood soaking into the front of his shirt. "I'll tell you what it makes you. It makes you a fucking idiot for messing with the wrong crazy bitch." She smiled at him. Even with his diminished vision, her teeth were impossibly bright. "Or just drastically unlucky," she added.

More coughing on his part, more blood spray. Between hacks, he mumbled, "I'm gonna make you love me."

He had no idea why he said it, where it had come from. A song maybe? He knew full well that he was becoming delirious.

"I'm sure," she said and disappeared for a while.

Scott was relieved she left, dropping his chin to his chest and closing his one good eye. For a while, he dozed, blissful darkness all around.

He didn't know how much time had passed when he woke again. The first thing he felt was cold. The first thing he heard was fabric tearing. He was annoyed at having his slumber disturbed. His head hurt and he was both thirsty and hungry.

When he felt his body jolt-a short, hard yank-he reluctantly opened his eye, looking down at himself. His chest was bare, streaked with dried blood, which left him wondering, but then he saw that his whole body was bare. The tearing and jolting had been Hailey cutting and ripping his clothing off, specifically his jeans and boxers.

"Wha tha fah?" His words were all fucked up. He sounded like his constantly shit-faced father. He knew he was alarmed at this development but the alarm was far away, a rocking rowboat on a distant horizon.

"How are you feeling, champ?" Hailey asked. She sounded cheerful.

"Thirthy," he said. His mouth seemed to be filled with glue.

"You want some water? I'll get you some."

She was gone again and Scott heaved the sigh of a much put-upon and exhausted man. His dry tongue probed the jagged remains of his front teeth and he felt panic begin to uncoil in his belly again. He struggled weakly against his restraints, hoping for the first time that this was just a very, very bad dream. He knew it wasn't, but still, he hoped.

Hailey returned, happily announcing, "Brought you your water."

He opened his mouth to say thank you and then his world exploded into blinding agony and he screamed instead. He screamed until something in his throat tore, but he barely noticed. Hailey shoved something-cloth-into his mouth, deep enough to gag him.

"How's your underwear taste?" she asked from another galaxy.

His one good eye, wide, watering and crazed, peered down into his lap. The sight of his genitals made him shriek, no longer just in pain now, but filled with sheer horror.

"That must hurt like a motherfucker," Hailey said. "Your skin is sliding right off." She chuckled a little. "Did you think I was bringing you a nice cold glass of water that I'd hold up to your chapped lips, quenching your thirst and maybe washing some of that crusty blood down your throat? My mistake. I should have mentioned I meant boiling water to dump on your pathetic excuse for a cock and balls." She laughed, sounding delighted.

Despite having damaged vocal chords-Scott knew this positively-he continued to scream as best he could. In his head, he was probably much louder than he was in reality, given that his mouth was full of his favorite Deadpool print boxers.

"Stop being so dramatic." Hailey had to raise her

voice, ensuring he could hear her over his shock and trauma. "It's not like I was gonna let you keep your junk anyway. You didn't actually think I would, did you? Soon, I'll flay the rest of the skin off with a potato peeler."

Scott began to hyperventilate. The room, her face, even her voice, fading to gray. A gray sound. How...? He hoped now that she would just kill him. If that was the only way to escape this nightmare torture, then so be it.

For a while, he drifted in and out of consciousness. He had no way of determining the passage of time. There were no windows in this basement. The only measurements of hours he possessed was how much pain he was in at any moment. Sometimes, the moments were fleeting, but mostly, they were not.

He sat, chained, in hi own shit and piss. He barely cared. The waste crusted between his ass cheeks and his legs, soaking the seat cushion beneath him, the foul stench barely registering in his nostrils. He was aware of the itch but that discomfort paled in comparison to the pain.

Hailey taunted him with blue Gatorade, teasing him, making him say please more times than he could count, making him beg as best he could. It went on for what seemed like hours until she finally relented, pulling the fabric from his mouth and dumping the liquid down his throat at a volume that nearly caused him to drown. He swallowed as fast as he was able, but squealed at the burn and vomited immediately.

"Tasty Windex, right?" She cackled as she shoved the boxers back into their permanent residence. "You truly are a fucking idiot. Pathetic."

He thought it was later that same day when she wrapped a plastic bag around his head, securing it with an extension cord, suffocating him repeatedly. Every time he was on the verge of losing consciousness, he prayed to die, but he came back over and over again, until she grew bored with that particular game.

Other times, it was just the cord and no bag. She yanked it as tight as she could, the muscles in her arms taut and rigid, hard ropes of steel beneath the human-like skin. She was in better physical condition than he himself was-much better than he'd first suspected upon seeing her all that time ago in the store, when he'd assumed she was far inferior to him.

He'd never given much thought to being strangled before but he discovered there was far more gagging involved than most might imagine. The underwear in his mouth was now crusted with old vomit tinged with blood but not too much. It wasn't completely unbearable as he'd learned to swallow it back down most times. At least until there was nothing left to vomit but his own bile.

Scott lived in a constant state of shaking terror. Hailey made good on her promise of the potato peeler, slowly scrapping the skin off first his penis, which he thankfully didn't remain awake for most of the time, but then his fingers and even his nose.

"Hold still, baby," she said, smiling at him with what seemed almost like kindness. "If you squirm too much I might slip and hit your eye."

He held as still as he could, which wasn't very because his body trembled uncontrollably, wracked with sobs and horror.

This isn't fair, his mind screeched. I didn't do anything that bad. I barely touched her. It's not fair!

He wanted to tell her that, to explain that her punishment did not fit his crime, but he couldn't. She was not a human woman, merely disguised as one. She was a monster, he now knew. A demon of some kind. It was fitting though, he supposed, as he was now no longer a man. Not in body, mind or spirit. He didn't know what he was anymore. Something less than an animal but it didn't matter. He was hers. He belonged to the demon and existed only to hurt. He was surprised whenever she called him by name, often forgetting that he even had one. Like now, as she spoke to him.

"You were right, Scott," she said sweetly. He regarded her dully, taking notice of the hammer she held in one hand, long, sharp nails in the other. "You said you'd make me love you and you were right. I do love you." She stuck three of the nails in the corner of her mouth but was still able to speak clearly enough to be understood. She placed the point of the single nail she held in her hand against the top of his head and hammered it into his skull. His head lolled forward with the impact.

"You helped me discover who I am," she said, taking another nail out of her mouth. "I'm grateful for that. Words can't express how grateful. But I can show you."

She hammered in the next nail, harder this time. Deeper.

"I'm going to keep you with me forever," she continued. "Or as close to forever as I can. Within reason, you know?"

Her voice no longer sounded like that of a demon. More like an angel, he thought. Another pounding on top of his skull. Through it. It was an odd sensation. He clearly heard the cracking.

"And to think," she said, lifting his chin with her free hand so he could gaze into her face. "It all began with a…" She trailed off. Or maybe he did.

He saw stars…

Gina Ranalli is the author of nearly twenty novels and novellas in the horror and bizarro fiction genres.

deadite
press

"Header" Edward Lee - In the dark backwoods, where law enforcement doesn't dare tread, there exists a special type of revenge. Something so awful that it is only whispered about. Something so terrible that few believe it is real. Stewart Cummings is a government agent whose life is going to Hell. His wife is ill and to pay for her medication he turns to bootlegging. But things will get much worse when bodies begin showing up in his sleepy small town. Victims of an act known only as "a Header."

"Punk Rock Ghost Story" David Agranoff - In the summer of 1982, legendary Indianapolis hardcore band, The Fuckers, became the victim of a mysterious tragedy. They returned home without their vocalist and the band disappeared. A single record sought by collectors, a band nearly forgotten, and an urban legend passed from punk to punk. What happened to The Fuckers on that tour? Why was their singer never seen again? No one has been able to say. Until now...

"Zombies and Shit" Carlton Mellick III - Twenty people wake to find themselves in a boarded-up building in the middle of the zombie wasteland. They soon discover they have been chosen as contestants on a popular reality show called Zombie Survival. Each contestant is given a backpack of supplies and a unique weapon. Their goal: be the first to make it through the zombie-plagued city to the pick-up zone alive. But because there's only one seat available on the helicopter, the contestants not only have to fight against the hordes of the living dead, they must also fight each other.

"The Book of a Thousand Sins" Wrath James White - Welcome to a world of Zombie nymphomaniacs, psychopathic deities, voodoo surgery, and murderous priests. Where mutilation sex clubs are in vogue and torture machines are sex toys. No one makes it out alive – not even God himself.

"If Wrath James White doesn't make you cringe, you must be riding in the wrong end of a hearse."
    -Jack Ketchum

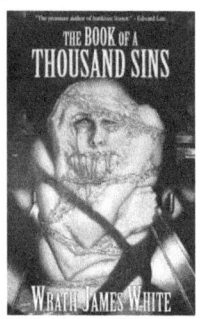

"Like Porno for Psychos" Wrath James White - From a world-ending orgy to home liposuction. From the hidden desires of politicians to a woman with a fetish for lions. This is a place where necrophilia, self-mutilation, and murder are all roads to love. Like Porno for Psychos collects the most extreme erotic horror from the celebrated hardcore horror master. Wrath James White is your guide through sex, death, and the darkest desires of the heart.

"Bigfoot Crank Stomp" Erik Williams - Bigfoot is real and he's addicted to meth! It should have been so easy. Get in, kill everyone, and take all the money and drugs. That was Russell and Mickey's plan. But the drug den they were raiding in the middle of the woods holds a dark secret chained up in the basement. A beast filled with rage and methamphetamine and tonight it will break loose. Nothing can stop Bigfoot's drug-fueled rampage and before the sun rises there is going to be a lot of dead cops and junkies.

"Survivor" J.F. Gonzalez - Lisa was looking forward to spending time alone with her husband. Instead, it becomes a nightmare when her husband is arrested and Lisa is kidnapped. But the kidnappers aren't asking for ransom. They're going to make her a star-in a snuff film.. They plan to torture and murder her as graphically and brutally as possible, and to capture it all on film. If they have their way, Lisa's death will be truly horrifying...but even more horrifying is what Lisa will do to survive...

"Genital Grinder" Ryan Harding - *"Think you're hardcore? Think again. If you've handled everything Edward Lee, Wrath James White, and Bryan Smith have thrown at you, then put on your rubber parka, spread some plastic across the floor, and get ready for Ryan Harding, the unsung master of hardcore horror. Abandon all hope, ye who enter here. Harding's work is like an acid bath, and pain has never been so sweet."*
- Brian Keene

AVAILABLE FROM AMAZON.COM

deadite press

"WZMB" Andre Duza - It's the end of the world, but we're not going off the air! Martin Stone was a popular shock jock radio host before the zombie apocalypse. Then for six months the dead destroyed society. Humanity is now slowly rebuilding and Martin Stone is back to doing what he does best-taking to the airwaves. Host of the only radio show in this new world, he helps organize other survivors. But zombies aren't the only threat. There are others that thought humanity needed to end.

"Tribesmen" Adam Cesare - Thirty years ago, cynical sleazeball director Tito Bronze took a tiny cast and crew to a desolate island. His goal: to exploit the local tribes, spray some guts around, cash in on the gore-spattered 80s Italian cannibal craze. But the pissed-off spirits of the island had other ideas. And before long, guts were squirting behind the scenes, as well. While the camera kept rolling...

"Reincarnage" Ryan Harding and Jason Taverner - In the 80's a supernatural killer known as Agent Orange terrorized the United States. No matter how many times he was killed, he kept coming back to spread death and mayhem. With no other choice, the government walled off the small town, woods, and lake that Agent Orange used as his hunting ground. This seemed to contain the killer and his killing sprees ended. Or so the populace thought...

"Suffer the Flesh" Monica J. O'Rourke - Zoey always wished she was thinner. One day she meets a strange woman who informs her of an ultimate weight-loss program, and Zoey is quickly abducted off the streets of Manhattan and forced into this program. Zoey's enrolling whether she wants to or not. Held hostage with many other women, Zoey is forced into degrading acts of perversion for the amusement of her captors. ...

"Answers of Silence" Geoff Cooper - Deadite Press is proud to present the extremely sought after horror stories of Geoff Cooper. Collecting fifteen tales of the weird, the horrific, and the strange. Fans of Brian Keene, Jack Ketchum, and Bryan Smith won't want to miss this collection from one of the unsung masters of modern horror. You won't forget your visit to Geoff Cooper's dark and deranged world.

"Boot Boys of the Wolf Reich" David Agranoff - PIt is the summer of 1989 and they spend their days hanging out and having fun, and their nights fighting the local neo-Nazi gangs. Driven back and badly beaten, the local Nazi contingent finds the strangest of allies - The last survivor of a cult of Nazi werewolf assassins. An army of neo-Nazi werewolves are just what he needs. But first, they have some payback for all those meddling Anti-racist SHARPs...

"White Trash Gothic" Edward Lee - Luntville is not just some bumfuck town in the sticks. It is a place where the locals make extra cash by filming necro porn, a place where vigilantes practice a horrifying form of justice they call deaddickin', a place haunted by the ghosts of serial killers, occult demons, and a monster called the Bighead. And as the writer attempts to make sense of the town and his connection to it, he will be challenged in ways that test the very limit of his sanity.

"Whargoul" Dave Brockie - It is a beast born in bullets and shrapnel, feeding off of pain, misery, and hard drugs. Cursed to wander the Earth without the hope of death, it is reborn again and again to spread the gospel of hate, abuse, and genocide. But what if it's not the only monster out there? What if there's something worse? From Dave Brockie, the twisted genius behind GWAR, comes a novel about the darkest days of the twentieth century.

AVAILABLE FROM AMAZON.COM

www.ingramcontent.com/pod-product-compliance
Lightning Source LLC
Chambersburg PA
CBHW060133260626
47160CB00005B/2088